The diary of
A YOUNG WEST
INDIAN IMMIGRANT

John, Mary, Clara, Joseph and Gloria
Many thanks for your contribution to this book.

I would also like to thank Devon, Victor and Rosaline,

Editor Louisa Sladen
Editor-in-Chief John C. Miles
Designer Heather Billin / Billin Design Solutions
Art Director Jonathan Hair

First published in 2001
by Franklin Watts
96 Leonard Street
London
EC2A 4XD

Franklin Watts Australia
56 O'Riordan Street
Alexandria
NSW 2015

ISBN 0 7496 4257 2 (hbk)
0 7496 4419 2 (pbk)

Dewey classification: 941.085

A CIP catalogue record for this book is available
from the British Library.

Printed in Great Britain

The diary of
A YOUNG WEST INDIAN IMMIGRANT

by Trish Cooke
Illustrated by Brian Duggan

FRANKLIN WATTS
LONDON•SYDNEY

ALL ABOUT THIS BOOK

This is the fictional diary of Gloria Charles, a young West Indian who travels from the island of Dominica in June 1961 to live with her parents in England. In the mid-Fifties and early Sixties many children from the West Indies came to meet their parents in England. It was a common practice for a child to be left with their grandmother in the West Indies, and sent for after the parents had found work and a place to live in England. This diary tells us the thoughts of a West Indian girl going through that experience. It covers her life from the age of ten to fifteen. It is based on a collection of real-life interviews with people who have had similar experiences.

A DIFFERENT LANGUAGE

The Dominican language – which Gloria sometimes refers to in the diary as "patois" – is a mixture of African, English and French words. Although this diary shows some of the different expressions and phrases that Gloria uses in her speech, to give the flavour of her original language, it has been written so that English-speaking readers can understand it.

24 APRIL 1961
GRANNIE'S HOUSE, 6 ROSE STREET, NEWTOWN, ROSEAU, DOMINICA

Marcia's eyes nearly pop out of her head when she see the book. It was my birthday last week, so when Grannie came home with the parcel after her trip to the post office, I knew it was for me. "This is a lovely book, " I said and I hug it and I hug it like I was hugging Mum, but really and truly the book is more real than Mum. If I'm honest I can't even remember Mum properly. All I have to go by is that photograph Grannie keeps on the wall of Mum and Dad. I can't see Mum's face clearly any more in my memories. But I know she don't forget us because I get a book.

The cover has a gold square at the top where it says NOTEBOOK. It looks important and when the sun shine on it, it sparkles. The rest of the cover is made up of my favourite colours, blue and green like Ma Veto's curtains. Grannie say she'll make me a blue and green dress just like my book. I'm going to keep my book under my pillow so I'll remember to write in it before I go to sleep.

25 APRIL 1961

I wasn't expecting Grannie to start making the dress so quick. She's making me a blue and green one and she's making one for Marcia, except Marcia's is not flowery like mine. Her dress is plain yellow. Grannie is singing in that angry voice of hers. Something's wrong. Last night she was sitting on the verandah smoking her pipe and looking up at the moon. Something's bothering her.

27 APRIL 1961

The dresses are almost finished. Grannie made us try them on to check the length. Grannie look sad about something, but Grannie not saying anything about anything. When I ask her she say it's big people business, but I know it's something to do with the letter that came with my parcel because since she read it her face change and she keep stroking my head. Grannie make me 'fraid when I see her so serious.

29 APRIL 1961

Marcia has been playing in my book. She's been

scribbling on the pages. What a mess! I told Grannie and she said if she don't behave she going to beat her. Grannie go and buy an exercise book from the store for Marcia, but Marcia still have her eye on mine. I don't blame her, mine is much prettier!

30 APRIL 1961

Grannie say come home straight from school, she have something to tell me, but after school Vince climb the biggest coconut tree and get us two coconut. We drink the coconut water first and after, Vince take a machete and crack the coconut open, and the white jelly look so wet and shiny in the sunlight. Mmmmm, I love coconut jelly! I like to scrape it out with my fingers, but Vince make two spoon out of pieces of the hard shell. We sit down by the sea to eat our coconut like we was King and Queen of the beach! The jelly was sweet! The water was so cool on my toes I had to take a little sea bath. I forget all about the thing Grannie say she have to tell me.

Grannie was vex when I reach home. She had the letter from Mum that came with my parcel and she ask me to sit down in her rocking chair on the verandah, to give me the news. As soon as she said I could sit in her chair, I knew what ever she had to tell me was a big thing, because as long as I have known Grannie, only Grannie alone has sat in that chair. Anyway the letter say I must go and meet Mum and Dad, take the boat to England, after Marcia's First Communion. I don't want to go. I want to stay here! I don't want to leave my Grannie and my Marcia! To go where? England? I don't even like the sound of the name of the place. I won't let them make me go! I won't!

WHIT SUNDAY, 4 MAY 1961

I wore my new dress for church. Marcia and me looked so nice. We were both wearing our white church hats and white gloves with our new dresses. I usually like Whit Sunday, but today's was spoilt because I know I'll be going away soon and this will be my last Whit Sunday in Dominica, maybe forever!

10 May 1961

I'm not sure how I feel. I haven't been sleeping
well lately. Mum and Dad have been in England
since I was six and I'm now ten. I can hardly
remember anything about them. Marcia's seven
and she can't remember them at all. Grannie is
all we've known for a long time and I can't
imagine life without her. Grannie says it's good
to go to England, but I'm not sure I want to go. I
keep looking at the photograph of Mum and Dad
on the wall, but their faces look like people I do
not know.

22 May 1961

After school Vince taught me how to climb to the
top of a coconut tree. I could see so far across the
sea. I tried to see England, but England is too far
away. Somewhere far... Full of strangers... I
wonder if they have coconut trees there? I
wonder if they have a beach like this one with
pebbles and stones you can use to skim the water
and watch them plop, plop, plop when you throw
them far. I'm the best at that, nobody can beat
me! And do they wash clothes in the river like we
do when we help Grannie, and do they let their
clothes dry on the hot stones when they spread
them out for the sun to heat them? I wonder if
they roast breadfruit and cashew nuts on an open
fire? And what will I do without Grannie there to
tell me scary stories when it's full moon?

3 JUNE 1961

It's Marcia's First Communion on Sunday. I go to
England on Monday. Although I'd like to see
Mum and Dad again, I want to stay with Grannie
and Marcia too. I really don't want to go to
England. I don't know much about the place,
only that lots of people keep going there and not
coming back. I don't want to go and not come
back. I want to stay here. Maybe if I tell Grannie
how I'm feeling she'll let me stay.

5 JUNE 1961

When I tried to tell Grannie about wanting to
stay in Dominica, she wouldn't listen. She said
Mum and Dad were waiting for me and that was
that. I asked her to come to England with me and
she said she couldn't. She said Marcia would
come to meet me soon, so I would not be on my
own there.

Marcia's not my friend. Hear what she say:
"You Gloria, it's always you that get all the nice
things!" I say, "It's not true," but she still behind
me shouting and making big noise saying,
"Mummy send you a nice book, pretty, pretty,
pretty and now it's you who is going to England!
Always you! Never me! You is the favourite!"

That burn me, you know, when she say that!
How I can be the favourite when all the time in
my heart I don't want to go at all? If I am the
favourite I wish Marcia would be the favourite

today and go to England instead of me! You see what Marcia don't understand is while I am with strangers she will be here with Grannie and all our friends on the savannah. Grannie knows everything about us. What if Mum and Dad have forgotten about me? What if they cannot remember the things I like?

Maybe I am worrying for nothing… Mum remembered my favourite colours are green and blue, she chose this book for me, so she must be thinking of me. She remembers I love writing so maybe it will be all right. But what about the things she doesn't know about me? Grannie has watched my tastes change… Mum doesn't know what I like for breakfast. She doesn't know I like cocoa and eggs every morning! What if we don't get on? I would rather stay in Dominica with the people I know. Maybe I'll suggest Marcia goes instead of me.

"Grannie!" I say, "Send Marcia to England nah?" Grannie just look at me. I think maybe she didn't hear so I ask her again, "Grannie…"

"Shhhhh" she say, and she put her finger over my mouth to stop me from talking, but I wanted to talk, I needed to talk.

"Grannie…" I say again and she squeeze my mouth between her fingers. It didn't hurt, but I make myself cry anyway.

"Why I have to go to England?" I say, "Marcia

11

want to go, send her!" Grannie wipe my tears with the hem of my dress, "Hush, baby," she say. "It's you they send for, so it's you must go..." and she rock me in her arms until I stop crying. Then I had another idea, "Grannie, what about if me and Marcia go together, we could keep each other company on the boat?" but Grannie shake her head. "And where your mother and father going to get the money from for the both of you to travel the same time?" I make my shoulders touch my ears. I don't know, and I don't care. Just don't make me have to go to that place by myself, I thought, but I didn't say it because I know how far to go with Grannie, so I shut up.

I think Marcia hates me. She keeps looking at me from the side of her eye, and when I turn to face her, she looks away. It's not my fault!

6 JUNE 1961

I've just finished cleaning Grannie's pipe. I love the smell. It's Grannie's smell. I wonder if I will remember the smell of the pipe when I get to England. When I put it down, Marcia picked it up and cleaned it again. She's trying to make me vex!

7 JUNE 1961

I've started to think of England a bit more now. Maybe it's not all bad. I've been told the streets are paved with gold, just like the label on my notebook. Imagine that! Gold streets, shiny and glittering. I told Marcia but she said she didn't care. I wonder if the roads are slippery, because I've heard too that sometimes the ground is so cold it turns to ice! I could move so fast that way. Yes man! Come see me sliding like a motor car! Yes, England might be fun after all!

8 JUNE 1961

"When you going, darling? Tomorrow?" That's what everybody kept asking me today. Marcia looked so pretty in her First Communion dress, but her face wasn't looking so pretty at all. She pull me aside and spat out the words like a snake: "Everything is you!" she say. "Today is my First Holy Communion, but it's still you, you, you everybody concern about!" She was vex!

I do wish she could see that this is a big thing for me. I'm excited and scared, both at the same time. My stomach is in knots and I don't know who to turn to. "It's not a bad thing you know" Grannie say. "You'll have a good, good time, you don't know how lucky you are!" And Marcia doesn't say a word even when I try to include her in my excitement. "When you come to England we'll…" I say, but she doesn't let me finish. She just walks away like I'm not even there.

I said some prayers with Grannie's rosary to see if I would feel any better. It makes Grannie feel better when she does this. I suppose I do feel a little better. Just a little bit.

When Grannie was packing my things I say: "Leave some things behind for when I come back!" But she just carried on putting all my things in the grip. "Don't be foolish" she said. Does that mean I'm never coming back?

I want Marcia to look at me and understand that I'm not leaving her because I want to, but she won't look me in the eye. I miss her already. Oh Marcia, we used to be so close... Today it seems we are so far away from each other and I haven't even gone away yet.

We've had so much fun together. Like the time we were hiding from Grannie and she didn't know we were hiding in the space under the house. I wonder if the houses in England are built on stilts like they are here? We hid there for such a long time: "Gloria! Marcia!" Grannie kept shouting, and all we could do was laugh and laugh, but we covered our mouths so she wouldn't hear. We could only see her feet passing by as she searched all over the street for us. You know, I nearly wet myself I laugh so much that day! It was so funny. Not so funny when she found us. Licks!

I'm writing this in our bedroom, sitting on our bed. Marcia is sitting on the floor opposite me and she's writing too. She never lets me see what she's writing. I want to talk to her but she won't look at me. Oh Marcia I wish you would look me in the eye and share these memories with me... just for today. But you won't, will you? I'll keep writing them down and maybe somehow I'll make you think of them, just as I am. I wonder if you know what I'm writing. Ha, I caught your eye! Was that a smile? Remember the time when we skipped school and took a sea bath and Grannie found our clothes in the bushes and took them home? We had to stay in the sea until dark because we didn't want people to see us running across the savannah naked.

Marcia, what about the time Grannie told us that story about Dad, the one when he was afraid... always that same old story! "Did I ever tell you about the time when your father was afraid?" she says, and then she looks at me and always says how much I resemble him when he was little. It's funny to think that Grannie is Dad's mum. "Look at you with those two big Cecil eyes," she says. Then she tells us the story again.

"Your dad was coming home from a party and he was taking the short cut through the woods, that's when he saw the donkey. Well I did warn him, you see, 'Cecil' I said, 'if ever you take the short cut through the woods and you see a donkey, don't you ever believe it is an ordinary donkey, oh no, what you see is not always what really is. I ever tell you about sookooyah? Evil witches? Well, that donkey is one of them, so you better run. But before you do, just to be sure it don't catch you, you have to ward off the evil spirit and the only way you can do that is by taking a hair from your backside and holding it up to the moon!" And when she tells us that story I always try to imagine Dad, the man who I resemble, running as fast as he could through the woods, with his pants round his ankles and a donkey chasing him: "He don't know what it was behind him," Grannie laughs. "He don't know if it was sookooyah, devil, witch or what – he just run!"

Sookooyah! That's what Grannie calls those bloodsuckers… I wonder if there's any truth in any of those stories. Witches, ghosts, spirits and things. I wonder if they'll be in England? What if I have a nightmare and Grannie's not there to help me sleep? Grannie always make joke and make you see the funny side of things. I like to see her laugh. I hope I never forget how she laugh. Maybe if I close my eyes I can save her laugh in my head.

Now I'm thinking of Dad… I wonder if we have the same face really. Maybe when I see him I will know him by my own face, looking at me from his face.

I think it's about midnight now. Earlier on, Marcia climbed into bed with me, she snuggled up when she thought I was sleeping. Now *she* is sleeping, I'm writing down the feeling because I never want to forget this warm and snuggly made-to-fit feeling. We belong together.

What if Marcia forgets me when I'm gone?

9 JUNE 1961
ON THE BOAT

The first thing I thought when I opened my eyes was – today's the day!

When I heard the first cock crow I jumped out of bed and I looked out of my window as I had promised Vince I would do. I saw his thin black legs move so fast over the dry dirt as he ran towards the house. I got up and went to meet him.

"Let me see you do it," he said when we reached the coconut tree and as he counted, one, two, three…I climbed. Before he reached eight I was back down again with my prize coconut held high. It was only then I noticed I had scraped my leg on the bark, sliding down so fast.

"Let's take a sea bath," Vince said, "the salt will do it good, make it heal fast!" So we went for a swim, and after he broke open the coconut we scraped the jelly out with our fingers. It wasn't as sweet as the first time.

"When I'm gone" I say, "Will you find somebody to take my place? Will there be a next girl climbing coconut trees with you?" But he doesn't answer straightaway, like he's thinking hard about the right thing to say.

"It won't be the same without you," he says, and I'm pleased he took his time to answer. I like Vince. I will write to him when I reach England. He promised to come and meet me in England, one day. Maybe I will be married with him when I get big.

About seven o'clock in the morning I got back home. Grannie was already up boiling the cocoa and making the eggs for my breakfast. She did not scold me for sneaking out so early. She just looked at me and stroked my head. Marcia hugged me and I thought I was going to die, die in England and never see Marcia or my grannie again! So I cried. Grannie kept saying, "Don't cry, don't cry!" but I couldn't stop.

Now I'm on the boat writing all this down. This is the first time I've had to write. What a day! Ma Burton, the lady I'm travelling with, is asleep so I have some time to myself. I'm feeling tired, but I can't sleep. I can't believe I may never see Grannie and Marcia again. But I will see Marcia again, won't I? Will Grannie and Marcia start to become strangers and will I hardly remember much about them? I'm frightened.

It was early morning when Samson, Grannie's friend, the man who sells the fish by the side of the river, came to pick us up in the truck. He had promised Grannie to take us to the harbour in Roseau if we needed a lift. I like riding in his pick-up truck. It has no roof on the back and Marcia and me enjoy the wind blowing our hair back. This morning Grannie and Ma Burton sat at the front with Samson, so when it drizzled, they didn't get wet. But Marcia and me didn't mind getting a little wet. It felt nice when the speckles of rain hit as the wind pushed against my face. We started to sing because we like to hear our voices change pitch when the next whip of breeze carries them off somewhere far. We wonder if someone passing by hears our song and knows we are the ones that sang it.

Marcia looks happy and sad at the same time. glad to be sharing my song and sad that this might be the last time. I was just sad. When we arrived at the jetty, my stomach dropped like a heavy stone. I didn't look at anyone in case I cried. I didn't want to cry. I wanted to be a big girl and let Grannie know I was going to be OK, but the tears were pricking at my eyes and I couldn't hold them in.

"Look" said Marcia excitedly, "There's your ship!" and when I did look up, I saw why she sounded so excited. It was a big white ship, called the *RMS Thistle*. That was written on the side of the ship, and I was going to be travelling on it, like a queen.

I held my head up high and caught Grannie's eye. She looked at me proudly. "All for you," she said, "That big boat come to take you across the sea to your Mammy and Daddy. See how special you are!" She gave me a big kiss and said, "Now you be good for Ma Burton and don't be talking nonsense in her head all the time. Keep yourself quiet and behave."

"I will, Grannie," I said and she rubbed my head. I hugged Marcia next and she held me tight until it hurt. We were one. When she let go, she didn't say anything, just closed her eyes tight and opened them again like we had seen big people do. Then she raised her chin and looked at me for a long time, like she was trying to remember me for always. I did the same.

Ma Burton took my hand and led me away from Marcia and Grannie. I'm travelling with her because she lives close by and today she's going to meet her husband in England. He went over there last year. We got into a little boat first, because the big ship couldn't come all the way to the jetty. And the little boat took us to the big ship. We had to climb up some steps on the outside of the boat. There was such a big gap between the steps, I thought I might fall through into the water below, but I didn't.

As I waved goodbye to Grannie and Marcia from the big ship, I said goodbye too to all the beautiful things I know as home. Goodbye beautiful river that flows through the centre of my small town; goodbye hills that I have run up and run down; goodbye parrot that squawks and talks; goodbye goats that stroll; goodbye crickets that scream and fireflies that light up my night! Goodbye music that makes my body bend; fruit that make my mouth water: mango; sour sop;

guava; goodbye passion fruit and my favourite, coconut jelly! Goodbye Marcia. Goodbye Grannie.

The two people that were so big in my life suddenly started to look small as the boat got further away from the jetty. Goodbye two dots! Goodbye! They never stopped waving. I believed they never stopped, even when I couldn't see them anymore.

I must have nodded off on my bunk bed, because when I woke up my book was still open on this page. It's been an exciting day. So many people on the ship. I've never seen so many white people – all the officers and the crew! I have never been anywhere before so I'm not sure what to expect. I'm feeling anxious. The movement of the boat is making me feel sick. I have never been on a boat before and I was not expecting to feel this way. Always moving. I don't know how I am going to manage. I hope I get used to it.

I didn't feel very much like eating but Ma Burton made me eat some bread and drink some tea to settle my stomach. She said tea is something that English people drink a lot of. I'm not sure if I like it. I feel so alone... Maybe if I write to people I can pretend that I am not alone, pretend they are with me. Yes, I'll write to all the people I miss and it will feel like they are still with me. I'll write the letters in my diary and when I get off the boat I'll copy them out and post them, and when I get

23

letters back, I'll stick them into my book. I'll stick everything that is special to me in here. Now who shall I start with?

6 Rose Street
Newtown
Roseau
Dominica

11 June 1961
RMS Thistle
On the sea

Dear Grannie,

The boat ride is not so good. I keep feeling sick and wish you were here to rub my belly and make me some proper bush tea to make the sickness go away. I love you and miss you already. I do feel very lucky though to get this chance to travel on a big ship to England. I am grateful Grannie, truly. I am seeing things I never imagined. I didn't know there was so much water in the world.

Your loving granddaughter,

Gloria

6 Rose Street
Newtown
Roseau
Dominica

15 June 1961
RMS Thistle
On the sea

Dear Marcia,

What mischief are you getting up to without me? Have you started to clean Grannie's pipe now? Ooooh, I miss that smell. You're not missing anything so far. The boat ride is going on and on forever. I'm not as sick as before, but when I get off it's going to be fun working out how to stop my body from moving around all the time. How am I going to manage on those icy roads?

Thanks for showing me how you really feel before I left. I will carry your hug with me wherever I go. I will write and let you know about everyone I meet and everything I do. You must do the same. Don't forget sisters share everything.

Take care of Grannie,

All my love,

Gloria

4 Riverside Road
Newtown
Roseau
Dominica

1 July 1961
RMS Thistle
On the sea

Dear Vince,

So much water. I'm sick of seeing the sea. That's all I see as I stare out of the cabin porthole. Sea, sea and more sea! I'm so much looking forward to seeing land. Any land. England has started to excite me. You know, the not knowing what to expect, the mystery, the adventure! And to see my mum and dad again will be strange, but I'm also looking forward to that now!

As I'm writing, it feels like I am with you. I already miss climbing the coconut trees. My legs won't miss it, though. The scabs are falling off now. I hope I get a scar, that way every time I look at it, I will think of you. Look after my little sister for me.

Love,

Gloria

1 JULY 1961

Ma Burton says we're here...
We're in **ENGLAND**! We've finally arrived.

6 Rose Street
Newtown
Roseau
Dominica

2 July 1961

8, Rows Nook
Buttershaw
Bradford
West Yorkshire
England

Dear Marcia,

I have to tell you exactly how it was the day I reached England, because although you are not here in flesh with me, I truly feel you are here in spirit!

Everybody was rushing to get off the boat and of course, me being so much smaller than the grown ups, I found that most of the time I was just getting caught up in the bustle and not moving that much at all. Ma Burton held on to my hand so tight and it was an exciting feeling to be part of all the rush going on around me, but when we got off the boat and started to separate, I started to feel the cold. My knees started to knock and all my mouth started to tremble. My teeth were clinking and clanking together and smoke, yes smoke, was coming out of my mouth, like a dragon or something! Ma Burton rub my shoulders with her hand to keep me warm and then somebody give her a blanket for me. And this is supposed to be summer?

I felt much better with the blanket around me. After Ma Burton had managed to find us a seat to wait on I started to look around. The first thing that struck me was how dark and grey everything looks, and how everybody, even the people who live in England all the time, even they hold on to their clothes for extra heat. They just seemed to be all folding themselves inwards, not walking straight and tall like we do back home.

I tightened the blanket around every bit of me, folding in the corners to stop the draughts coming in, and I was using Ma Burton's thigh like my pillow (you know how cuddly she is), but before I got real comfortable and into a deep sleep, I heard a stranger's voice asking Ma Burton something. A deep voice, and when I looked up, there he was, grinning, just like the picture at home on Grannie's wall!

It was Dad! The real flesh and blood Dad! I could hardly believe he was real!

Love always,

Gloria

P.S. I didn't want to tell you this but I think I have to... Mum really did forget about us and now she has a baby instead. His name is Michael. He's three years old. How could they do this to us?

3 JULY 1961

That baby Michael – who does he think he is? He thinks he's so cute! He can't even say my name! Glo Glo! That's how he says Gloria. He cannot even talk properly! He always wants me to pick him up and hug him. I want him to be Marcia. I miss my sister!

26 JULY 1961

Mum is so pretty. She hasn't said much to me. She just keeps looking and studying my face. I think she likes me, but I'm not sure. I feel a bit more comfortable with Dad – I feel I know him more from Grannie's stories. And he *does* look like me. Sometimes I want to ask Mum things but I am not sure where to start. She looks so tired. I had cornflakes with COLD milk this morning. Yuck!

28 July 1961

6 Rose Street
Newtown
Roseau
Dominica

8, Rows Nook
Buttershaw
Bradford
West Yorkshire
England

Dear Marcia,

Finally I have some time to myself. Sister, dearest, when I tell you what is what you won't believe! Well, when I reached the house – no, let me tell you from the start...

Dad collected me from a place called Southampton and brought me to a place in the north of England called Bradford. There are lots of big stone buildings in the town. They look like castles. I wonder if the royal family live in one of them? On the bus ride over to Mum and Dad's house I noticed the land is very similar to Dominica in some places. Bradford has lots of hills and the landscape is beautiful in its own way but the colours are not as bright. There are some pretty flowers, but I didn't notice any hibiscus. Everything looks dull. I miss the bright greens and the blueness of the sky in Dominica. The days here are grey, even when the sun is trying to shine through, and there's a peculiar grey cloud that comes out of the tops of the houses. I have just found out this is the smoke from the fuel they burn inside the houses to keep warm.

In the house where I am staying the rooms are very big and the heat does not stay in the room. It's very draughty. "Shut the door, shut the door!" That's all I hear, and yet back home we are always asking for the door to be left open so we can get some air. I have caught a cold. Even now, I'm sneezing. We have paraffin heaters in this house. Dad doesn't like the smell. "Don't sit too close to the heater," he says to me because I'm always sitting right close up to the heat. He's always moving me away. "Mind you don't burn yourself," he says. You know, I almost did, but he caught me in time. It's good that he did, as I might have knocked it over and caused the house to catch on fire!

The other night Dad was so tired he started to doze off in front of the heater but the air was thick with fumes and when he woke up all his nose was full of black soot stuff. He could hardly breathe. He called for Mum, "Iola! Iola! I cannot breathe!" and Mum soaked a rag in warm water and wiped away the black soot from his nose. It was scary.

"Cecil, why you fall asleep in front of the fire," she say. "You want to be dead?" And Dad just looked at her like it was a stupid question. "Yes..." he say, "I want to be dead..." but he was smiling and I knew he didn't mean it.

I could see in his eyes he was only pretending. Dad jokes like Grannie, sometimes. He makes you feel better.

Dad works very hard in a factory. They make steel there. When he comes home from work he is always so tired. Mum is working part-time in the hospital. She cleans there from four o'clock until eight o'clock. That's when I look after Michael. Dad comes home at six o'clock, but all he wants to do when he gets home is eat and rest. I don't know how they managed without my help. Mum couldn't work then, you see. With the money from her job now, they want to save up to get your ticket.

I am so looking forward for that day!

Love always,

Gloria

30 July 1961

Mum and me haven't had much time alone together since I reached here, because Michael takes up so much of her time and when she's not with Michael she's working. Today when she was plaiting my hair she took her time, like she wanted to talk. It felt good feeling her fingers grease my scalp and play with my hair. I didn't cry at all when she combed through the knots. Mum wears her hair in cane rows in the house, and when she goes to work she puts on this European hair wig. It's made up of short brown curls. She let me try it on. It looks pretty.

In the house Mum speaks patois, but outside the house she speaks English. Posh. I like to hear patois, man. It reminds me of home. If I open my mouth and talk patois, Mum tells me I have to talk English. She says I will get on better at school if I speak English all the time. It upset me because my voice is already changing. Even though I am trying hard to talk the same way I did back home, I am finding myself talking like the children in the area. I can hear myself turning into a Yorkshire lass. Then I have to laugh!

Mum said she is going to take me shopping tomorrow to look for some school clothes and shoes. I am to start school in September. She showed me the school. It looks so big. I am sure to get lost just trying to find my way around it. I wonder if the children there will be nice?

2 AUGUST 1961

I went shopping with Mum the other day. Although we went to find school clothes we did not get any clothes for school. I saw so many styles in the windows and Mum tried on some clothes. She looked like a model. Mum bought me this beautiful dress. It has orange velvet on the top and a white pleated skirt that sticks out like a fairy. I like to spin around in it. She bought me some T-bar shoes as well. She said I can wear the new dress to church next Sunday. We're going to look for school clothes again next week.

3 AUGUST 1961

Mum and Dad were arguing last night. I think we spent too much money on clothes.

"We hardly have any money as it is!" he say. "And I hear the foreman say they will be laying people off! I might not even have a job!" They both look worried.

15 August 1961

We went shopping again. This time Mum and me went straight to the school uniform shop. I can talk to Mum a little easier now. I took the opportunity to ask Mum some questions that have been burning me.

"When you and Dad came to England," I said, "why did you leave Marcia and me behind? Was it because you didn't want us any more?" Her eyes filled with tears and she caught her breath.

"Didn't want you?" she said in disbelief. "Of course we wanted you. That's why we came here in the first place, because we wanted to make life a little bit better for you." I listened carefully, for both me and Marcia. "Things just were a little harder than we expected," she went on. "Your dad and me had to find work, so we could afford a place to live, and that took a lot longer than we thought it would. And then Michael came along and so we needed more time to save up... Plans don't always go the way you want them to," she said and her eyes looked like they were not looking at me at all but thinking of something else. I like Mum. She never forgot about us. She just had other things on her mind.

I got my school uniform. I have to wear a tie – It's green and yellow and red – just like our Dominican flag!

Mum said education is the most important thing, and that is one of the reasons she came to England, so that we could get a good education. I'm teaching Michael the alphabet, the way Miss

Williams showed us. He sings it well. He's a quick learner!

16 AUGUST 1961

I received a letter from Marcia today! I'll stick it into my diary. That way I'll never lose it!

8 Rows Nook
Buttershaw
Bradford
West Yorkshire
England

18 July 1961
6 Rose Street
Newtown
Roseau
Dominica

Dear Gloria,
 I am glad you arrived in England safely. I miss you too. I can't believe we have a brother! Who does he look like? When will Mum be sending for me? I can't wait to come to England. Nothing has changed here. I am finding school to be boring nowadays. Miss Williams beat me yesterday because I took my shoes off in class – but you know how hot it does get sometimes in the classroom. I just slipped off my shoes under the table, and the prefect must have crawled under the table and brought them to her. As you can expect, Grannie was not pleased with me! Oh, Grannie sends her love.

Your sister,
 Marcia

P.S. Grannie says to make sure you grease your hair well because the coldness might break your hair. She say don't follow the white girl's fashion as our hair is different to theirs.

7 SEPTEMBER 1961

On the first day of school, although part of me had been looking forward to going, I found myself telling Mum I was sick when it was time for me to go. I really did feel sick. My stomach was churning. Mum introduced me to the teacher and the teacher, Miss Grinstead, made a fuss over me. I just wanted to be invisible and not draw too much attention to myself, but Miss Grinstead took a liking to my hair and wouldn't stop touching it. The more she commented on my hair, saying how soft and fluffy it was, the more the other children wanted to have a feel. There were lots of them, all putting their hands in my hair and saying they wished theirs was as soft. (They wouldn't be saying that if they had to comb it with those combs that have the teeth so close together!)

16 SEPTEMBER 1961

I asked Mum to press my hair, and when I went to school my hair was looking straight. I just wanted to blend in and not be different, but then everybody noticed that my hair was straight and Miss Grinstead asked me what I had done and I told her Mum had pressed it. When she asked me to explain and I told them how Mum heats the iron comb on the stove and combs it through my hair, the whole class looked at me in horror. I tried to explain that I kept still so it didn't burn.

But they all looked at me with
pity like my mum had done
something bad. There was only
one girl who understood.
Her name is Barbara.
She's from Jamaica.

25 SEPTEMBER 1961

I can't believe how different school is over here!
The children do not listen to the teachers. At the
nuns' school in Roseau the teachers were always
strict. Mum said she brought me here for a better
education but I'm not so sure she's done the
right thing. There seems to be no discipline.

The children do as they please and there seems to be no set time for when the work has to be done. Mum has asked me where my homework is but there is none.

I'm bored. I spend all day doodling and sketching things I remember about home, because I never want to forget! Every lunchtime though, I sit in the library and read. I like reading some of the history books, and books about different countries. I still think about home a lot.

The funny thing is, even after all my daydreaming and doodling, I am still ahead of most of the children in my class.

30 SEPTEMBER 1961

Barbara started at the school in July, just before the summer break. I am so glad she is from the West Indies too. She didn't say much to me at first but I could tell by how she looked at me that she was my friend. She has the kind of eyes that look like she is wanting to laugh all the time, but her mouth stays shut. Except when we're alone and then Barbara doesn't shut up! I can tell we're going to be good friends.

18 OCTOBER 1961

When Barbara talks about Jamaica she makes me think of home. I will never forget about Dominica. England can never be my home!

25 OCTOBER 1961

The half-term holiday has only just started and I am already bored. Barbara and me have a skipping rope and we've been singing:

London Bridge is falling down
Falling down
Falling down
London bridge is falling down
My fair lady.

Just like Marcia and me used to do at home. I wonder who Marcia plays with now?

26 OCTOBER 1961

Barbara and me have been playing elastic twist

with some of the girls on our street. Two of us put the elastic around our ankles and one girl has to jump in and out of the elastic and skip around it.

There's this game we play with tennis balls too. We throw the balls on the wall and catch them and sing songs like:

Over Mother Brown
Over Mother Brown
Over, over, over, over
Over Mother Brown.

I'm the champion!

There's a girl called Linda who lives at the end of the road, she's nearly as good as me! We were playing skipping, Linda, Barbara and me.

Sally in the kitchen
Doing a bit of stitching
In came the Bogey man
And knocked Sally out!

Right in the middle of the song, Linda's brother threw a stone and it got Barbara just under her eye. Craig's always troubling us, calling us names and things. Barbara's face was all bloody with the stone that catch her face, "Big bully!" I shout and I throw a stone after Craig but he ran away. Later Barbara's mum went to Craig's house and told Craig's mother what he had done, but she didn't seem to care. Barbara's mum went mad!

Linda still plays with us but when her brother is around she pretends she isn't with us. Linda said Craig will tell her mum. Her mum has told her not to play with us. I don't like Linda hanging around with us anymore because she is only our friend if no one sees her with us. I would rather she played with someone else but I don't know how to say it to her.

Dad said to Mum that he'd been reading something in the paper about the colour bar. I'm not sure what it is. When I asked Dad he said that some white people don't like black people and they're not letting them in to certain places. I think that's silly.

6 November 1961

Everywhere smells of smoke today. Last night was Bonfire Night. I've never seen anything like it. A weird custom that English people do! They light big fires in their back gardens and put a man doll on it. Something to do with English politics. There was this man called Guy Fawkes who tried to blow up the Houses of Parliament a long time ago. They send off fireworks in his memory. The black sky fills with colourful lights. It looked really pretty. I had to watch from my bedroom window because Mum said it was dangerous to go out, in case somebody wanted to get ignorant and throw the fireworks about. Everywhere stinks today!

12 November 1961

A Jamaican man has started delivering West Indian food to our house. He brings everything – yam, plantain, sweet potato, green banana, dashin. Every time I see him he makes me laugh (he doesn't have any teeth) but I don't want him to see me laughing so I hide my face in the cushions.

4 December 1961

It's really cold, but there's no sign of snow. It will soon be Christmas. I hope we have a white one. I am trying to imagine what snow will be like. I keep opening the fridge and looking at the white stuff in the freezer bit where the ice cubes are. When I scrape it it makes my fingers numb. Is that what snow feels like? I'll have to put lots of clothes on when I go out to make my snowman. See me nah... I'll roll the snow into a big ball and then make a head for it like those snowmen on Christmas cards. I really can't wait. I hope it snows soon.

5 DECEMBER 1961

Mum and Dad were talking when we were eating our supper. "The Immigration Bill is coming into force early next year..." Dad said.

I'm not sure what it is but Mum looked frightened. "We must send for Marcia before it becomes too difficult to get her into the country," she said, and my stomach started to churn. Was this Immigration thing going to stop me seeing my sister? I felt really worried. Then Mum said to Dad, "Why does life have to be so hard?" and she started crying. Moments later she was in the bathroom being sick. "I think it's the saltfish," she said. "It doesn't seem to agree with me these days, and when I was back home, that's all I ate!" Dad rubbed her back and tried to make her feel better but she didn't look good. And since Mum was in a bad way already, I suppose he didn't think his news would make matters any worse. "Bad news," he said, "I wasn't sure how to tell you, but they might be making me redundant at the steel works." But when he said that, Mum nearly spewed her guts out. When Dad saw me listening he said, "Don't worry, Chicken, everything's going to be all right," and he smiled at me, his big daddy smile, but I'm worried. I hope Marcia comes really soon!

6 DECEMBER 1961

"When will Marcia..?" I started to ask. Mum was stroking my head. "Don't trouble me with your questions now, Gloria," she said and then she started singing and rocking gently from side to side, with my head on her lap:

Ave, Ave, Ave, Maria
Ave, Ave, Ave, Maria...

Immaculate Mary, our hearts are on fire
Mmmmmm mmmmmmmmm..."

I felt comforted like that, with her watching over me. She looked comforted too.

"When you can't do it yourself," she said, "you have to rely on God." She reminded me of Grannie praying with her rosary. "I've tried," she said, "but it's out of my hands..." " Then she started to pray in a whisper, "Sweet Jesus, hear my prayer..."

9 DECEMBER 1961

We've got new neighbours next door. They're an Irish family. There's a girl, the same age as me, called June. I asked her if she wanted to play with us and she said yes. She looks like she could do with a friend. She lives with her grandmother. I've not seen her mum yet.

June has a whip and top. She showed me how to spin it. We chalked lots of colours on to the top and now when it spins all the colours blend into one. It looks really pretty!

11 DECEMBER 1961

An awful thing happened today. Michael was playing with my marbles and he put one in his mouth and nearly choked. Dad had to thump his back until the marble came out. We thought he was going to die. I didn't realise how much I love him until now. I was getting vex before when he was playing with my things, but now I don't mind as long as he doesn't hurt himself. I'll make sure I put anything that might be dangerous up high.

18 DECEMBER 1961

At the weekend when Dad is not working, Mum and Dad have friends round at the house. It's great hearing patois. It's like being in Roseau, when the old men play dominoes outside the rum shop. This is the only time I see Mum and Dad relax. Barbara and her mum and dad come to the house too but they don't speak Dominican patois. Our patois has got lots of French words in it. Barbara and her mum and dad speak Jamaican patois – it's got more English words in it. It's so funny having to translate the French into English when Mum and Dad get carried away and think they are back at home!

19 DECEMBER 1961

I am teaching Michael to read. "C-c-c-c-c-cat," he says and he's only looking at the word. I cover the pictures with my hand. He's not even four yet. He's so clever. "Glo Glo," he says, "read me a story." I enjoy reading to him. I even like how he says my name now. It's special. He's the only one who calls me Glo Glo.

20 DECEMBER 1961

I can't believe it! It's actually snowing! Big white soft pieces of ice falling from the sky and sliding down the window. Mum says I can't go out and play in it because I am just getting over a cold, so Michael and me have been watching the other children play. June keeps calling for me and waving at me through the window. She and her brother are making a snowman. I want to do that!

I sneaked out the back door and played in the snow with June. Boy, if you did see me throwing snowball! I even roll in the snow. Now all my clothes are wet. Mum's pretending she never saw me but I heard her muttering: "They that don't hear, must feel!"

All my nose is blocked up with cold. Every minute I'm sneezing. Mum keeps giving me that look that Grannie used to give me sometimes. Mum just finished rubbing me down with Vicks. Oh, it stinks!

CHRISTMAS DAY, 1961

I woke up feeling cold. I had a dream about Marcia. She was in England with me but we weren't living together. She was in one of those high-rise flats and I went to visit her, but the lift was broken and I couldn't get to her room. I stayed outside the building waving up at her window but she didn't wave back... I miss her so much.

Mum put lots of Christmas presents under the tree so when I came downstairs I had a look to see which ones were mine. One was a doll, a big blonde blue-eyed doll, the same as the one she posted to Marcia last month. It walks, if you hold on to its shoulders. I think I'll plait her hair later.

Mum cooked turkey, roast potatoes and sprouts. I've never had turkey before. I didn't like it much. Dad asked her why she didn't cook some rice and peas and chicken but she said turkey at Christmas is an English custom.

Dad fell asleep in front of the telly after dinner. Mum played Jim Reeves and country and western records, Michael played with his new toys and I plaited my new doll's hair.

I miss Grannie today. I could do with a hug from Marcia. I would give anything to smell that pipe.

Maybe Grannie will come to England with Marcia next year. It will be 1962 next week!

1 JANUARY 1962

Last night Mum let me stay up. We watched a
Scottish man wearing a kilt on telly. He was
dancing over some swords. I wonder what
Grannie and Marcia are doing now…

22 MARCH 1962

I haven't written in my diary for a while. But I
notice now that Mum's putting weight on. She
says she has to put her feet up. I think Mum
might be going to have another baby. Oh no! If
having Michael meant it took longer for them to
save up to send for me, then will having
another baby mean waiting even longer for
Marcia to come over?

5 APRIL 1962

Got a letter from Vince! He's going to live in
America. I'll stick it into my diary and keep it
forever.

8 Rows Nook
Buttershaw
Bradford
West Yorkshire
England

22 March 1962
4 Riverside Road
Newtown
Roseau
Dominica

Dear Gloria,

I have to write to you and tell you of my plans.
I have been getting straight 'A's at school since
you left. I suppose I have had nothing to take my
mind off studying. The coconut trees are full! I
won a scholarship and my parents are sending me to
the States to live with my aunt so that I can study
there. I had been hoping that I would come to
England to study, but it seems not. I hope you are
enjoying your time in England.

Love,
  Vince

P.S. Dominica has been at a standstill since you
left, and no next girl has taken your place.
When I settle in the States I will send you my
address.

MAY DAY, 1962

On Saturday there was a fête at the school. Some
children decorated their bikes with crêpe paper
and they had a procession in the street. I wanted
to be part of the fun. "Can I have a bike Mum?"

I asked, but I knew as soon as I said it I was being selfish. How could Marcia come to England quickly if I wanted all Mum and Dad's money for myself? Mum just shook her head. "Money's a bit tight at the moment," she said and I suddenly began to wonder if Marcia would ever come to England.

11 MAY 1962

At school we all danced around this pole with lots of colourful ribbons dangling from it. They called it a Maypole. A girl called Brenda got to wear a crown. She was the May Queen. I wish I could be the May Queen.

21 MAY 1962

I'm having to help a lot more around the house. Mum is always tired these days. How can she have another baby when Marcia is still in Dominica! What can I tell Marcia! Her letters always ask me the same thing...

When will Mum and Dad be sending for me? How many more months will I have to wait before I can share the adventure with you?

Perhaps I will spend my next birthday with you all. Have they mentioned a date?

Tell Mum I am looking forward to the hugs and kisses I know she is saving for me...

It seems you too have forgotten me. You do not write as often as you used to. Weren't you the one who said sisters should share everything? Why the sudden silence? Why have you deserted me? Have you forgotten your roots, where you come from? Remember, I am your sister...

I never know what to write in my letters to Marcia, because nothing I can say will help. I understand how Marcia feels, but I cannot help her. There is nothing I can say to ease her pain. It's not my fault she is still in Dominica, but knowing Marcia, she will be putting the blame on me.

There's nothing I can say or do, so I write to her less and less, and only mention the good stuff. It seems Marcia is turning into a thing of the past and my present is oh so different. I feel sad about her.

12 JULY 1962

I brought a good report home from school. "You're so clever," Dad said. "You make me proud, girl, you know that?" It was good to see him smiling, and nice to know that I had put that smile on his face. Too many days he looks like he is worrying about something, and when he's not worrying, he is just tired. "With all those brains," he said, "you'll be able to choose the job you want to do, not like your old daddy who has to take any job the white man give him just to get by." Dad was so proud, he gave me ten bob. (I don't think Mum saw.) I think I'll treat myself to the pen set I saw in the corner shop window.

4 AUGUST 1962

So busy! Mum needs all the help she can get these days because she is so tired. The baby could come any time. The doctor says she has high blood pressure so she cannot do too much around the house. I have to do it instead.

27 AUGUST 1962

I hardly have time to write in my diary these days. I've been doing all the cooking and looking after Michael, as well as going to school. I'm so tired.

4 SEPTEMBER 1962

Really tired.

8 SEPTEMBER 1962

I have a new sister. She was born early morning on September 5th. Her name is Nancy. I picked it out myself. She's so lovely. When I rock her in my arms she snuggles up warm. As soon as Mum finishes feeding her, I pick her up. Mum says I will spoil her, but I don't care. She's such a sweetheart. I love her. Love her. Love her.

I want so much to share her with Marcia but I can't write and say anything nice about Nancy – I know Marcia will get upset and say that I have betrayed her. But it's not my fault! Even though I have a new sister, I'll never forget Marcia, and I'll always miss her! Always!

11 SEPTEMBER 1963

I can't believe a whole year has gone by since I last wrote in my diary. The baby (she's no baby any more), little Nancy, is walking now. She's into everything. You can't put anything down without her interfering with it. She's so funny. I take her almost everywhere with me – I just put her in her pram and walk her around the block and I chat to her. She looks like she understands. I've told her all about Marcia, but I didn't really tell Marcia much about Nancy, in case she minded. Nancy's so cute, like a little doll. Michael started school last week and he already knows how to read. *I* taught him!

5 JANUARY 1964

I've been so busy, I keep forgetting to write in my diary. I've just been making room for Nancy in my bedroom. She's going to share with me now. I've been clearing away some of my junk. I find it hard to throw things away. My suitcase can be the special place for all my important stuff. I'll put all my things in there.

3 AUGUST 1965

I am fourteen years old now. Seems like ages since I last wrote in here, and boy, how life has changed.

I came across this diary whilst going through the old suitcase I travelled with when I first came to England. My intention was to throw out some old junk, but I can't throw any of this out. This is all a part of me, and although I'm not the same as when I first came here, it's good to be reminded where you come from. And I want to write in my diary again.

There's so much in here from my past. Fond memories. Old photographs from home and stamps I tore off letters from Marcia and Vince. Oh Vince, I wonder how life is turning out for you. You never did send me your address in the States. As for me, I never thought I would settle here in England, but I have. Once I had found a friend, Barbara, life was more bearable. Her mum and dad are very similar to mine. They came to live in England in the late Fifties and then Barbara's older sister came out here; Barbara and her brother followed soon after. The only difference is Marcia is still not here, but Barbara has become like a sister to me. We do everything together.

I still think about Marcia, though. I'm

fourteen now so she'll be eleven. She'll be different now to how I remember her. I wonder if her face has changed? And Grannie. I wonder if she still looks the same? Same lines where her eyes and her mouth turn up when she laughs? And will she sound the same? How did she sound? Oh please *please* let me remember her laugh. If I keep looking at the old stuff, maybe it will come back to me...

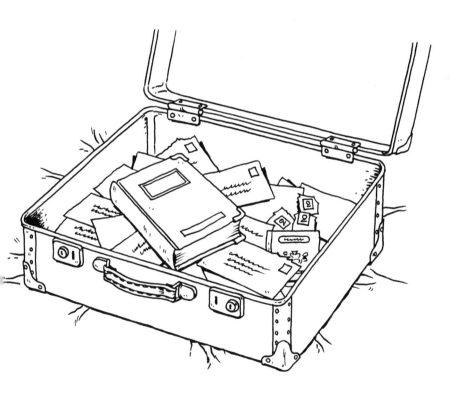

4 August 1965

More stuff… old photographs.

Me and Barbara! I remember when we took these. In that photo booth in town. Two years ago… yeah, about two years ago.

Barbara came with me to bring the sub money for Mrs Fevrier. Barbara's mum calls it "pardner". I don't know if it's an island thing, two different names for the same thing. Anyway "sub" or "pardner", it's a way of saving money. Lots of West Indians do it. A group of friends save an agreed amount of money every week and each week a different person gets the lump sum that everyone has put in.

It was pouring it down with rain, and on the way back from Mrs Fevrier's, we stopped off at the photo booth to keep dry until the bus came. I'll take this photo with me to the youth club tomorrow, embarrass her, see if she remembers…

5 August 1965

I took the photo of me and Barbara to the youth club today. She remembers! She told me to hide it quickly in case "you-know-who" saw it. She really likes him. I wonder if he'll ask her out. We were talking in the toilets and that record came on...the one I brought to school at the end of term. *Lightning Strikes*, that's it. Lou Christie sings it. And then this lad comes in to the lasses' toilet and says "Steve wants to dance with yer..." So she just went off and danced with him all night. I wasn't bothered really because she's been wanting him to ask her for ages. I prefer to dance on my own, me.

I like Ska music and blue beat. *One Step Beyond*, I love that one, and *C-A-P-O-N-E, Don't call me scarface. My name is Capone, Al Capone.* And, boy, when the music take me, when I take the dance floor, there's no stopping me. Honest, I'm in a world of my own. That's what Barbara says. It is true. I don't really notice anyone at all.

There's lots of West Indians at the youth

club. We've got a proper little family thing going. There's Renald and Renaldo, Trevor, Gordon, Danny, Clayton, Randolph, Oria, Joan, Sylvie, Monica, Claudia, Virginia, Gwenneth, Mary, Clara and they're from all over – Dominica, Jamaica, St Kitts, Nevis, Antigua! We have such a laugh. We all came over here around about the same time, and although we are all from different parts of the West Indies we still have so much in common. I can't wait until next week!

12 AUGUST 1965

We did our usual again. I haven't got any fashionable clothes, so I left the house in a pair of long pants and a pullover. By the time we got to the youth club, however, both Barbara and I had changed into our good clothes.

Barbara's big sister's got so many clothes, Barbara managed to sneak out a cute green minidress for me and a neat pale pink dress suit for herself. I put rollers in my hair last night so my hair had an extra bounce. This evening I gave myself a fringe and combed up the bit behind to give it more body. And then I sprayed loads of hair lacquer on it to keep it in place. Mum bought me one of those vanity cases for my birthday so I brought it with me and put my pullover and long pants in it.

Barbara's got some pale lipstick so we put some of that on and we both looked so grown-up. We always make sure we wipe it off before we get home though or else we know what we'll get, "What kind of warpaint you put on yourself?" or "So you think you is a big woman?" or "You want to flaunt yourself in public? Cover yourself up, girl!"

"Be back in the house for ten!" Dad always says. Hardly worth going out, but if we time it right, and we always do, as soon as the last record has finished we can run up to Sunbridge Road and catch the quarter to ten bus home. We take the short cut through the Rec. and get home really quickly!

Well, Steve and Barbara danced together all night again and I did my own thing. I was twisting the night away when this white boy I've never noticed before started dancing in front of me. He was sort of dancing on his own and sort of dancing with me. I pretended not to notice but there's not many white boys come to the youth club, so it wasn't like he was invisible.

It was while this boy was dancing in front of me that Danny came from nowhere and asked me to dance. Danny's never asked me to dance before, so I knew it was only because the white boy was moving in. Danny's a bit prejudiced. I don't know why he lets himself get mixed up in all the bad talk about white people. If you don't get to know somebody how can you say they are all bad? I thought the white boy was cute and I was curious to know what he was really like. I danced with Danny, but all the time my eyes were on the white boy. When the record finished, the white boy did a strange thing. He came over to where I was dancing with Danny and said "Thanks for the dance," just like that, "Thanks for the dance." I could have choked laughing, but when I looked at him good, I could see he was quite cute. He had his hair combed real nice.

All night this boy kept looking at me when I was just doing my own thing. I could feel his eyes on me. It wasn't a bad feeling. I liked it. Kind of reminded me of when Vince used to look at me back home. Then that Sam Cooke record came on:

> *Another Saturday night and I ain't got nobody,*
> *I got some money 'cos I just got paid,*
> *Oh, how I wish I had someone to talk to,*
> *I'm in an awkward way...*

And he walked right over from where he was standing and asked me to dance. Oh Mama, and he danced real good. Slow and close up. I thought I was going to faint. I could feel everybody looking, but I didn't care. I've never danced up close to a boy before and I didn't mind one bit.

Afterwards he said "Thank you" and went to meet his friends. I didn't get a chance to talk to him after because that was the last record. Barbara and me had to run for the bus. I don't even know what his name is. But I want to know!

14 AUGUST 1965

I can't stop thinking about the white boy.
Barbara said he lives on the estate behind the
garages. It's a bit rough up there. Mum's always
telling me not to go up that side. I wonder if
he's lived there long?

19 AUGUST 1965

The white boy wasn't there tonight. I had made
myself look extra nice. Barbara had managed to
sneak out some false eyelashes her sister had in
her make-up box. She put them on for me. They
made my eyes look like that singer, Dusty
Springfield's. All wasted, he wasn't there! I
couldn't dance that good, anyway, because the
shoes Barbara lent me were a bit big and the
point at the front went on and on. I kept
tripping over them. My feet are killing me.
I hope he comes next week.

26 AUGUST 1965

Mum and Dad are going out. I can't believe it! They never go out! Why tonight? I have to babysit! I won't get to see him. Oh man! What if he is looking for me to dance with?

27 AUGUST 1965

Barbara said he was there, but she's not telling me everything. I can tell she's hiding something. But the more I ask her the more she says that as far as she knows he was there alone. That probably means he was there with a girl.

28 AUGUST 1965

Barbara's sister found out about us using her clothes. Barbara's mum said she can't go to the youth club anymore, which means I can't go either, because I've no one to come home with. I'll never see **HIM** again! I'll go out of my mind...

9 SEPTEMBER 1965

As it's my last year at school Miss Smith, the Careers Officer, was talking to us about jobs today.

"So, Gloria, what are your plans for when you leave school?" she asked me pleasantly.

"I don't exactly know, Miss Smith. I reckon I want to be something that means I can help people, specially people who weren't born in

67

England, like me. Perhaps I could learn to be a lawyer?" I said. She was going through some papers on her desk, but when I answered her she looked up quickly. "You want to be a *what*?" she laughed. So I repeated, "A lawyer, Miss Smith, so if there's any advice you can give me to help me achieve this I would..."

She stopped me there, "I'm sorry, Gloria, but I think you are a bit out of your depth," she said and she took out some leaflets. "Here," she said handing me a list of local factories. "Most girls like you," she said, "can get a job quite easily in one of the wool factories." "But Miss Smith," I interrupted, but she wouldn't let me continue. "I haven't got time for this," she said. "I've got lots of children to see, so I can do without your cheekiness." But I wasn't being cheeky, I just wanted to know what I needed to do to become a lawyer. But she ushered me out of her room, so I had to leave.

Next week I'm doing some work experience at the wool factory. Mum said, "It's good that you will be working soon, a little extra money coming in will be a big help." Should I start work soon? In the wool factory?

18 SEPTEMBER 1965

I started work experience today. I was just walking around with the others, looking in all the departments and watching the workers and all of a sudden I saw **HIM**! I couldn't believe it. The supervisor said, "Oh, you know each other, do you? That's useful, since Ian's going to be showing you how to pull the knots out of the yarn!"

I smiled at Ian and Ian smiled at me, and he shuffled up and made room for me on the bench. When I sat next to him I could feel my face getting hotter and hotter. All the windows were open and normally I would have felt cold, but next to Ian I was roasting. There was a table covered in cloth and he was running his hands over it.

"Like this," he said, "You just put your fingers on here and feel where the knots are and then mark 'em with this chalk." I did what he said, put my hands on the cloth, but I couldn't feel a thing. I felt numb. I just kept wondering if my hair was all right and if my nose was shining. If it was, he didn't say anything.

"You missed a knot," he said. "Feel, there's another!" He put his hand on top of mine and pressed my palm down on to the cloth. "You have to be firm or you'll miss where they are," he said, and I was thinking about how firm his grip was on my hand and wishing he could keep it there forever. But the bell went and everyone stopped for a break. *Shucks!*

20 SEPTEMBER 1965

He said I can ask him anything I need to know. He's talking about the job, of course. All I want to know is, "Has he got a girlfriend?" Barbara thinks I should ask him, but I think it's forward for a girl to ask a boy these things. I see him at the bus stop when I'm going home and I can't seem to talk, I just smile. I think he wanted me to sit next to him on the bus but I felt awkward and sat near the back. I'm not sure if he likes me... I mean *really* likes me, or if he's just being nice.

4 OCTOBER 1965

I saw him at the bus stop with this girl. They were laughing together. He stopped when he saw me and waved. I waved back.

9 OCTOBER 1965

I saw him with that girl again. They were linking arms. Oh well. I really thought he liked me.

13 November 1965

Barbara and me have started going to the youth club again. Same crowd. No Ian. I guess that's all over then. I'm quite sad about that…

19 November 1965

I've been offered a job in the wool factory. They wrote to me saying I could have a full-time job there once I leave school. I'll be leaving school at Easter next year. I really fancied my chances as a lawyer but it doesn't seem to be possible. Wasn't it Dad who said that with my brains I would be able to choose what job I would like to do, unlike him? So why does it feel like I have to go for the wool factory job, when I would like to do something else? That doesn't sound like a choice to me.

I feel annoyed because I don't know how to become a lawyer and no one is giving me any information. And then there's Mum: "Life will be so much easier with more money coming in!" Easier for who? Don't I have a say in this? It's my life…

But then I think I'm being selfish. I mean, the money I will be able to give to Mum, will help her save for Marcia's fare. Who do I think I am anyway, wanting to be a lawyer? I've decided to write back to the manager at the factory and say that I'll take the job.

1 DECEMBER 1965

Just posted a Christmas card to Grannie and Marcia. Marcia's eleven and a half now – I don't think I'll recognise her when I see her again.

8 DECEMBER 1965

I heard today that June and Linda will be working at the wool factory and they start the same day I do. I wonder if I'll see Ian and how I'll feel if I do?

17 December 1965

We got our Christmas cards from Grannie and Marcia this morning. It's really strange but I've got so used to the way of life here (something I thought would never happen!) I think I like it as much as home. If I had to make a choice between England and Dominica, I don't know what I would do. I would love to see Grannie and Marcia again, but if I went back for good, I don't know if I would fit in there now. A lot of the friends I had there have moved either to the States or London. I don't know if I could live in Dominica again. I would miss Mum and Dad, Michael, Nancy, Barbara and all my friends at the youth club.

18 December 1965

Mum's been grinning all day. She's up to something.

19 DECEMBER 1965

There's a Christmas dance at the youth club on Saturday. Mum asked me what I wanted for Christmas and I showed her this trouser suit I had my eye on in a shop window in town. It's pale green with a waistcoat. When I tried it on Mum said it suited my complexion. She bought it for me as an early Christmas present. That's what I'm wearing on Saturday. I can't wait to show Barbara!

31 DECEMBER 1965

Mum just showed me her building society book. She's finally saved enough money for Marcia's fare. She'll be coming here by aeroplane in April. What an adventure! I really will see her next year! She'll be here for my birthday.

2 JANUARY 1966

I wonder what Marcia will think of England? And of me?

10 JANUARY 1966

I've been clearing out the room Nancy and I share. Dad's throwing out the old double bed and we're getting a bunk bed for Marcia and me. I'm getting the top. Nancy's bed is going to be against the wall. It's going to be a tight squeeze.

Michael has his own room still – that's the bonus of being the only boy!

I'm not sure how I feel about Marcia coming here. In a way I've got used to her not being around. I still want her to come but I hope she fits in and doesn't upset everybody because I know how she does get sometimes if things don't go her own way. I didn't mean it like that, I just mean...Things are going to change when she arrives. I hope she likes Barbara.

11 JANUARY 1966

Mum posted the letter today to tell Grannie to start getting things moving their end.

16 JANUARY 1966

What a year 1965 was! I feel like I'm grown-up. I suppose Marcia will have changed too. I hope she likes it here. It took some getting used to, but finally England is home sweet home.

14 FEBRUARY 1966

Guess what! I got a Valentine card!

It came through the post. I keep opening it and looking at it over and over. The person has cut out the letters: L-O-V-E from the newspaper and put them inside my card. It gives me goosebumps thinking about somebody thinking

about me that way!
I don't know who it is.
I pass people in the corridor at school and
wonder if it's them. I'm looking closely into the
eyes of everyone at the youth club but, nobody is
giving anything away. Sometimes I daydream
and hope it's from Ian, but I've got a feeling
Barbara is having a joke on me. I hope I'm wrong.

27 FEBRUARY 1966

We still haven't heard back from Marcia and
Grannie. I hope everything is all right at home.

4 MARCH 1966

I got a letter from Marcia…I'm going to stick it
into my diary, that way I'll always remember
what it said.

8 Rows Nook
Buttershaw
Bradford
West yorkshire
England

14 February 1966
Newtown
Roseau
Dominica

Dear Gloria,

I received your letter, but it seems I am not meant to be in England. Not long after the letter arrived, Grannie took sick. I thought at first it was because of the letter, that she did not want me to leave her, but she really is sick and it looks bad. She spends most days in bed and her temperature runs high night and day. I would not feel right leaving her like this. Gloria, she calls your name often, and I was wondering whether you could perhaps take a trip over here? I fear it is very serious.

Please make haste with your reply,
Marcia

I wrote back straightaway, telling her I would do my best to get there as soon as I had managed to get the money together for my fare, but Mum said, "Gloria, you must go now," and she took the money she had saved from the bank and paid for me to go. I could see Mum was sadly disappointed that she would not be seeing Marcia. I asked "Would you like to go instead of me Mum? That way you can let Marcia know how much you miss her and next year when we've saved enough money I'll see her too."

Mum just smiled, "Thanks darling," she said. "But I think Marcia and Grannie want to see what kind of beautiful woman you have grown up to be," and before I could answer her she said, "because that's what you are." And she gave me a kiss.

"But what about you?" I asked her after that, and she said "I'm your mother and no matter what it looks like, I get my pleasure from doing what I think is right for my children, so go and enjoy yourself with your sister," she said. "You have waited long enough."

8 MARCH 1966

I'm writing this from the aeroplane. I'm feeling afraid. Afraid of what I might find when I reach Dominica. I can't believe I allowed myself to forget about my family back home. What if Grannie is too sick to…I don't even want to think about it.

I have forgotten Grannie's laugh, I can't hear it, not even when I close my eyes.

When I said goodbye to Mum last night, I was seriously wondering whether I would return to England. Who was I trying to kid? I'm not English, I never will be. Dominica is my home, and I belong with Grannie and Marcia. I feel as if I've missed out on so much, growing up here. I wonder if Grannie still loves me the way she used to. Even when she was mad at me, she was never mad at me for long. She'd always make a joke of things, and laugh… that laugh.

We're approaching Dominica now. We're flying over water. I can see the beautiful green landscape, the rough edge of the coast and the lush green hills. Oh, it's good to be back! No one can take this away from me, it will always be mine, no matter where I am.

9 MARCH 1966
GRANNIE'S HOUSE, NEWTOWN, ROSEAU, DOMINICA

It's evening. I'm sitting on the verandah, writing poetry.

Oh that smell!
That fertile smell.
All my senses have come to life again. Everything
looks so much clearer
The blue sky,

79

The greenness of the land,
The bright colours.
My skin is being caressed
by a soft warm breeze.
The sound of patois teases
my ears,
And the sweet pulp of mango massages
my throat and melts
on my tongue.

Heaven...
I've died
and gone
to heaven.

Alone on the verandah I write.
Watching the fireflies pierce the night
with their warm bright glow.
Listening to the crickets
and their high-pitched screams
Calling – "You there!
Gloria!
Where do you belong?"

I thought everything would be the same
the same as how I'd left it,
but I was wrong.

9 MARCH 1966

There was this young woman waiting in
Arrivals. A beautiful woman, full of life,
bursting with joy, her face animated as she
chatted to one of the customs officers, and then
she turned, saw me and gasped, "*C'est soeur
moi!*" and ran towards me, her arms wide open.
I couldn't breathe with all the kisses, and I
didn't want to ever again, because her kisses
were enough for me.

"Gloria! Gloria! Gloria!" she screamed and I
answered "Marcia! Marcia! Marcia!" in
response, kissing her back and back and back.
Oh, how I had missed her. How I had managed
to get by without her for so long, I will never
know. My sister! My sister! Approaching twelve
years old, but already a woman…

She held on to my arm and steered me
towards a pick-up truck that was waiting to
take us home.

"Come, come" she said putting her head
against my shoulder – oh how she'd grown,

legs long like coconut treetrunks – I laughed.

"Where you going with those legs?" I said, and slapping her behind I said, "And what's this!" Her figure had developed into that of a woman, even before her years. She just moved my hand and put it around her waist, giggling, like the child I remembered, and said, "It's mine, all mine!"

The ride home was a bumpy one, along dirt tracks that still had not been made into roads with the dry dust rising in the heat. "How is she?" I found myself daring to ask, "Grannie, how is she doing?"

"Since she heard you were coming," Marcia smiled, "you know Grannie, she pulled herself out of bed and tried to make like nothing was wrong. She wants to see you so bad!" I felt better knowing she was up and about, but I knew Grannie enough to know that it didn't necessarily mean she was well.

The old lady was sitting on the verandah, waiting when we approached. Rocking back and forth in that chair of hers, and smoking her pipe, deep in thought. I didn't want to disturb that image, because that was exactly how I remembered her. I just stared and stared and thanked the Lord.

When the truck stopped, so did the chair, and she stood up slowly to watch me jump down, her arms outstretched, her smile beginning to show now, grinning so wide, a deep chuckle stirring within, waiting to erupt.

"Whoi! Whoi! Whoi!" that's all she said,
"Whoi! Whoiii! Whoiiiii!" and the screams got
louder and longer. I didn't know if she was
going to laugh or cry and since her legs looked
so frail and thin now, I ran as fast as I could one,
two, up the wooden steps to where she stood
waiting for me to fill her arms.

And she wrapped me in them.

"Grannie! Oh my grannie, it's good to
be home!"

Cornmeal porridge with nutmeg, I'd dreamed
about it. Only Grannie makes it taste the way I
love it. I ate it until I was bursting, but then still I
ate some more. Picked mangoes from the yard
and filled my belly until I felt sick, but I didn't
care. I just felt hungry and wanted to be filled
with all of the Dominica I had missed. Tired, I
threw myself into the shower and then sat down
on the verandah and wrote poetry.

13 MARCH 1966

I really don't want to go back. I love it here. It
feels like I never left. It's good to walk barefoot
again and feel as your feet clasp the earth – you
really and truly belong where you walk. Grannie
just looks at me. Doesn't say much, just nods her
head in approval. She looks at me different now.
Does not look on me as a child. I can see in her

eyes she sees me as a grown woman. And I look at her, and I see my grannie still.

14 MARCH 1966

"Soooooooooo," she said. Grannie has this way of talking. You know straightaway what she's going to say as soon as she begins. I knew she was going to ask me about my life in England, but I didn't want to talk about it. I wanted to put all that behind me.

"Sooooooooo," she said again, "Tell me about England." I shrugged my shoulders and her arms opened up, calling me in. I obliged.

"Any boyfriends?" she said, and I blushed.

"Grannie," I warned, but she had a twinkle in her eye that showed me she was teasing. I told her there had been someone I quite liked called Ian and she asked me if he was English and I nodded. She chuckled, "My Gloria is an English girl." She laughed but I took offence. "I'm Dominican," I said, defending myself.

15 MARCH 1966

I went to the market today by the riverside and I could hear some boy trying to get my attention. "Psssssssst! Psssssst! Hey, English girl!" he called.

I never turned around, but I knew it was me he was calling. What's happening? Am I changing colour? Am I walking with a different rhythm? Is it my voice? What? When I told Grannie, she just chuckled and she and Marcia

looked at each other, with a shared expression.
Do they really see me as an English girl too?
How can I convince them I'm not?

17 MARCH 1966

Marcia has grown up so fine. She is not the same
girl I remember. She is no longer bitter or
resentful towards me – quite the opposite. I think
she has learned to value what she has here,
recognising it was me that missed out on this
glorious country. I love it here, but I almost feel a
stranger and I envy the familiar way Marcia
walks down the road, smiling and waving at
everybody she knows. When anyone stops and
talks to me they seem friendly, but a little distant.
Do they feel like I betrayed them too? I am *not*
English! Why can't anybody see that I am still
the same Gloria? I must talk to Grannie, maybe
she will help me to know who and what I am.

18 MARCH 1966

Grannie laughed when I tried to explain how I
was feeling. She wasn't being mean, she was just
acknowledging she knew what I meant.

We were out on the verandah. Then she sat
me down on her lap, wrapped her arms around
me and asked me what I could see. I could see
the sun going down – a bright red and yellow
sunset filling the sky and gradually sinking
down below the horizon. I told her I saw the sun

setting, but she shook her head and asked me again. I didn't know what she wanted me to say, so I said nothing. She asked me again and I shrugged my shoulders: "Grannie, I see the sun going down after a long day!" I sighed.

"Is that all you see?" she asked me.

I looked again at the radiant sky and immediately felt a sense of wonder, amazed at how the mix of colours had warmed the sky. No one colour could take all the glory, because each ray of light needed the other to truly shine. It didn't make sense, and yet, for that moment, everything did.

Grannie looked into my eyes and said, "Child, go back to England, and make a difference!" and her words, followed by her deep, low laugh, will always stay with me, because I knew what she meant. She wanted me to make use of the choices that my mum and dad had made available to me. She wanted me to be *all* that I could be. All of me shining, nothing less.

7 APRIL 1966

I wasn't ready to go back to England, but Grannie said "Don't worry about me girl, I'm fine. I was only sick because I didn't know how you was settling in England."

"I sent letters" I said, "You knew I was OK."

"True, you sent letters, but letters are just written words, and I needed to see your eyes to know how you truly felt," she said.

"And how do I feel?" I asked opening my eyes wide for her to look inside and see my soul. And she laughed as she leaned forward and pinched my cheeks like she was peering into the whites of my eyes. "You feel like a child," she said. "But I can see you're a woman. You'll be all right," she whispered.

Marcia didn't even pay us no mind. She looks so content and at home with herself.

"Next year then" I said to her, " It'll be your turn to come to England, next year", but she shook her head. "No Gloria, I'm not coming to England. I'm happy where I am. Maybe I'll come for a visit, but I'm not staying." I couldn't persuade Marcia to come to England, and when I looked at how happy and content she was, I didn't want to.

Before I left I promised Grannie I'd go and get a good job, and I promised both of them I'd visit often.

8 APRIL 1966

I arrived in England last night, and it felt good to be back. There was a warm reception waiting for me in the airport – Mum and Dad; Michael and Nancy; Barbara, and a fantastic surprise! A handsome West Indian gentleman calling my name in a strong American accent. **VINCE**!

It was Vince!

"How…? How did you get here?" I asked .

"I've been living in England since February," he said. "Didn't you get my Valentine's card?"

And I was supposed to know, instinctively,
I suppose, that the card was from him! "Why
didn't you get in touch and let me know you
were coming to Bradford?" I asked. "Because I
wanted to surprise you," he said putting his arm
around my shoulder. "Now didn't I surprise
you?" he said kissing my cheek, and I blushed. It
was the best surprise of my life, but I didn't feel
ready to tell him that yet!

Over dinner Vince talked and talked,
    "... and when I got the letter from Leeds
University to say that I had been accepted and I
looked on the map to see how close I would be to
where you are, I was very pleased." He looked so
pleased to be here. I watched Vince speaking and
enjoyed watching his mouth form the words.

He has soft, full lips and when he's speaking he wets them with his tongue a lot. When he stopped speaking I was lost because I hadn't heard his question. "Huh?" I said, but I knew I sounded dumb because Michael started teasing me.

"Glo Glo? Why have your eyes gone all goo-goo?" he asked and then he laughed, "Goo-goo Glo Glo!" and everybody laughed with him, even Vince, but I didn't mind. Vince has a dimple on his right cheek. It's only there when he laughs. Funny, I never noticed it before.

He looks so well. All grown-up now. A man. Who would have believed we were the same kids that climbed coconut trees together?

"I've got something to show you" I said, when all the others had gone to bed and Vince and I were the only two up, or so I thought. Then I heard Dad clearing his throat. "It's getting late, Gloria" was all he said, and I knew that he was telling me to go up to bed, but before I did I showed Vince the little scar on my right leg. It was still there, a part of me and it would never go away. "I remember when you got that!" Vince said. We smiled at each other. "Goodnight," I said, and he gave me such a long tender look I thought he would never reply, but he did, ever so softly, "Goodnight," he said.

9 April 1966

I was supposed to start my job at the wool factory today, but I didn't go. Miss Smith didn't give me the right advice. I intend to find out how to go about becoming a lawyer, and if not a lawyer then something more fitting to me. Vince said he will show me around the University in Leeds and maybe I can get some information there.

One thing I do know is, I am going back to school after the Easter holidays to sit my exams and then once I get the results I'll take it from there.

Grannie, thanks to you, I'm ready to be the best that I can possibly be. I'll use the richness of my two cultures and make the most of the choices my parents have made available to me...

I'm ready to make a difference.

FACT FILE

THE WEST INDIES

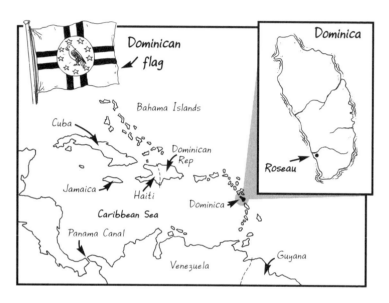

Dominican flag

Dominica

Bahama Islands

Cuba

Dominican Rep

Jamaica

Haiti

Roseau

Dominica

Caribbean Sea

Panama Canal

Guyana

Venezuela

FACTS ABOUT DOMINICA

The original settlers in Dominica were the
Arawaks and the Caribs from South America
(Amerindians). There are no Arawak descendants
in Dominica today, but Caribs still live in a section
of Dominica known as the Carib Territory.

The Europeans, Spanish, French, English and
Dutch all came to Dominica to discover and take
over new lands as European colonies. European
plantation owners grew coffee, cotton, tobacco and
sugar cane crops there. The new plantations needed
labourers and so slave traders went to Africa to

capture people there. They brought them back to the Caribbean to sell them to European plantation owners as slaves. Fortunately, in 1884, slavery was abolished and in 1978, Dominica gained full independence from the United Kingdom.

CARNIVAL

Carnival is an African and French festival. It's a time for enjoying yourself, music making and dancing in the street. In the olden days people wore masks to the carnival. The French word for mask is 'masque' and so people attending the carnival were called 'masqueraders'. The Notting Hill Carnival is a festival that has travelled from the West Indies to England. It is celebrated in London every year at the end of August.

DANCE

The dances performed in Dominica have a strong African influence. The traditional dances, such as *Be le*, originated in Africa. But French and British influences can also be seen there – in such dances as the quadrille or the heel and toe.

RELIGION

Christianity is the main religion in Dominica. There are three churches in Roseau, the capital: the Methodist church, the Roman Catholic cathedral and the Anglican church. In the book, Gloria's grannie and her mother are both Roman Catholic.

BRITAIN AND THE WEST INDIES

WHY DID THE FIRST WEST INDIANS COME TO BRITAIN?

When the West Indies were among the colonies owned by the United Kingdom, this meant the people who lived in the West Indies were also citizens of the United Kingdom.

The first migration of West Indians to Britain began after the Second World War. West Indian servicemen who had fought for Britain returned to the West Indies, but found it difficult to go back to the lives they had lived before. Many of them came to England because it felt more familiar to them than their original homes in the West Indies.

WHY BRITAIN?

Britain was known as the "mother country", and because Britain had colonised the West Indies, some West Indians went to Britain for work. Most West Indians thought they would be back in their own country after a few years having saved enough money to set themselves up back home, but as the years went by this was not always the case. It was very difficult to earn enough money to go back home and start again there. And sometimes England became home to the West Indians who had settled there.

How Did the first West Indians Travel to Britain?

Some of the first West Indians to go to England travelled on a ship called the *SS Empire Windrush* in 1948. The journey lasted twenty-seven days!

In the Fifties and early Sixties many West Indians travelled to England by boat. In the mid Sixties more people travelled to Britain by plane.

Where did West Indian Immigrants live?

The first West Indians to come to Britain lived in shared rooms. Living accommodation was very expensive. Later on, some Caribbean immigrants put money together so that they could buy their own houses. A few immigrants qualified for council housing.

Why did Parents Leave their Children?

Parents often travelled without their children so they could secure jobs and housing before settling with their families. It was about 1960 before children started coming to England to live with their parents.

What Was the Immigration Bill?

The Immigration Bill was drafted in November 1961 and passed as law the following February. It was put in place to limit the numbers of immigrants to Britain. In 1961 many immigrants came to the United Kingdom in an attempt to beat the ban.